How to draw Trucks and Tractors

Rebecca Gilpin

Designed and illustrated by
Stella Baggott, Non Figg,
Erica Harrison, Sam Meredith
and Jan McCafferty

Contents

Delivery trucks

To make a scene like this, paint a road and road signs after you've painted the truck.

1. Mix some yellow paint and a little water on an old plate. Then, paint a rectangle on a piece of white paper, for the truck's trailer.

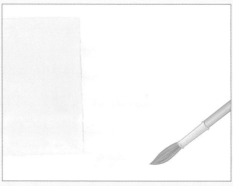

2. Use blue paint to paint a cab at one end of the trailer. Then, add a curved shape at the bottom of the cab, for a mudguard.

3. When the blue paint is dry, paint three black wheels at the bottom of the truck. Add a safety bar, between the wheels, like this.

You could draw a truck with a low-sided trailer filled with plants.

PETE'S PLANTS

Draw a handle on the door.

4. Leave all the paint to dry. Then, outline the truck with a black felt-tip pen. Draw around the mudguard and add a door, too.

5. Draw a side-view mirror on the cab, then draw a driver. Fill in the driver with felt-tip pens. Then, draw a logo on the side of the trailer.

6. Using a thin silver pen, add hubcaps and bolts on the wheels. Then, fill in the mirror and the door handle, too.

Dump truck

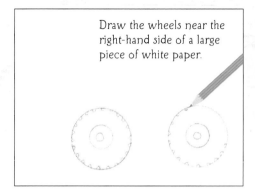

Draw the wheels near the right-hand side of a large piece of white paper.

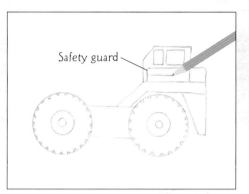

Safety guard

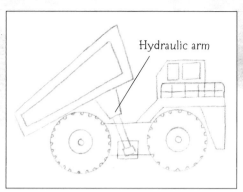

Hydraulic arm

1. Draw two big circles for the wheels. Add a hubcap on each wheel. Then, draw lots of tiny half circles around the wheels, for the tread.

2. Draw two lines between the wheels and a big mudguard over the front wheel. Then, add a cab, with windows and a safety guard.

3. Draw a line for the bed, above the back wheel. Then, add the rest of the bed above the line, and add a hydraulic arm below it.

To do a big scene like this, draw diggers and trucks in the background.

When you've drawn
over the outlines, add
a driver in the cab.

Draw lots of bolts
and rivets on your
truck and its hubcaps.

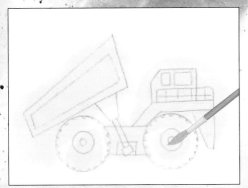

Pull a finger over the bristles
of the brush, like this.

4. Using a clean paintbrush, brush water over the paper. Dip the brush into watery yellow paint and blob it onto the truck and hubcaps.

5. Blob watery black paint onto the truck's wheels. Brush some swirls for dust clouds, too. Then, leave all the paint to dry.

6. Splatter black paint over the dust clouds with a dry paintbrush. Roughly outline the truck with a black pen, then erase any pencil lines.

Tanker truck

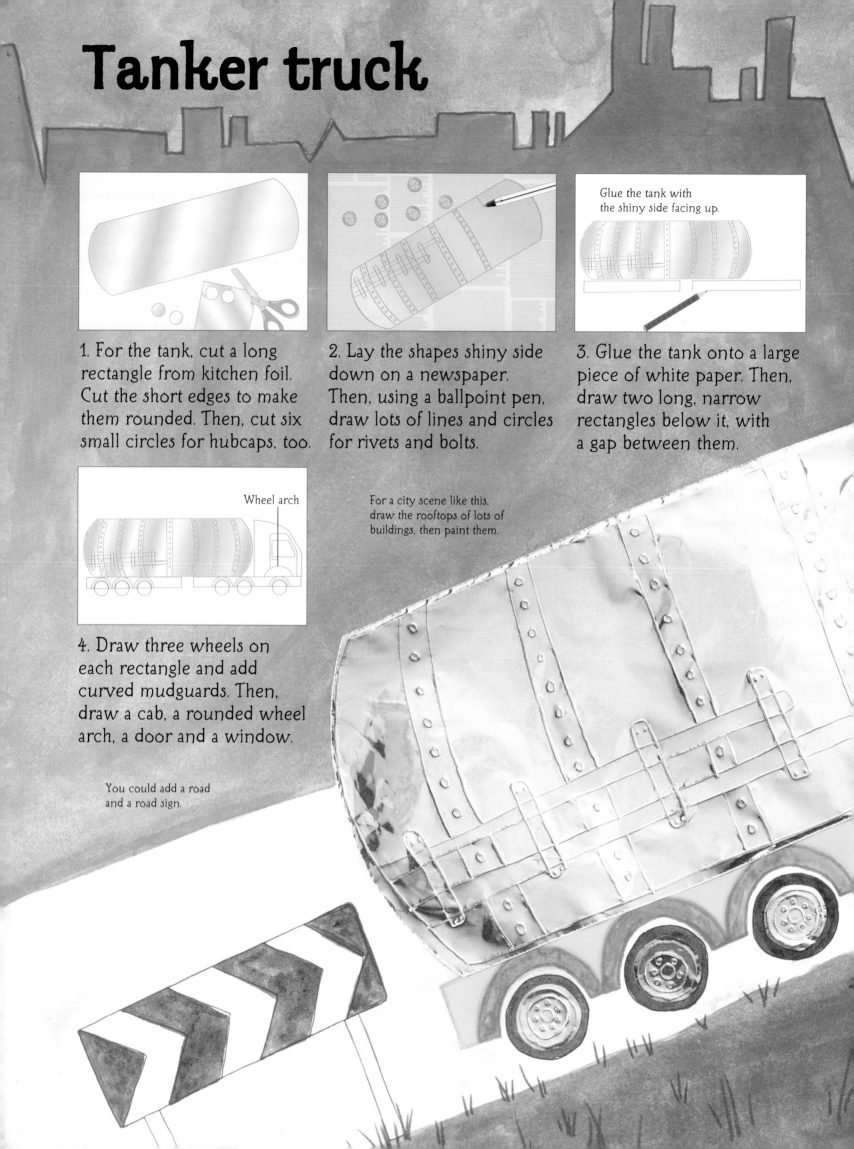

1. For the tank, cut a long rectangle from kitchen foil. Cut the short edges to make them rounded. Then, cut six small circles for hubcaps, too.

2. Lay the shapes shiny side down on a newspaper. Then, using a ballpoint pen, draw lots of lines and circles for rivets and bolts.

Glue the tank with the shiny side facing up.

3. Glue the tank onto a large piece of white paper. Then, draw two long, narrow rectangles below it, with a gap between them.

Wheel arch

For a city scene like this, draw the rooftops of lots of buildings, then paint them.

4. Draw three wheels on each rectangle and add curved mudguards. Then, draw a cab, a rounded wheel arch, a door and a window.

You could add a road and a road sign.

5. Draw a driver, then add a radiator grill and another window. Then, fill in the truck with watery paints and leave the paint to dry.

6. Outline the truck and driver with felt-tip pens. Fill in the driver with pens, too. Then, glue the foil hubcaps onto the wheels.

7

Big red tractor

You could draw a trailer behind the tractor, too.

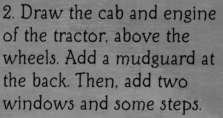

1. Using a pencil, draw a big circle for the tractor's back wheel. Add a smaller circle for the front wheel, then join them together with a line.

2. Draw the cab and engine of the tractor, above the wheels. Add a mudguard at the back. Then, add two windows and some steps.

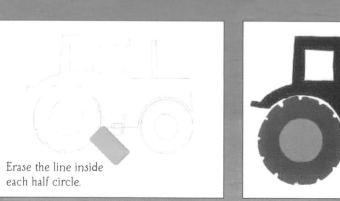

Erase the line inside each half circle.

Ledge

3. Draw a hubcap on each wheel. Then, draw lots of tiny half circles around the wheels, for the tread. Add a funnel on the engine, too.

4. Fill in the cab and engine with thick red paint. Paint the tractor's wheels and stack, then fill in the steps and hubcaps, too.

5. When the paint is dry, draw over the outlines with a black pen. Then, draw curved lines for the mudguard, and a ledge above the steps.

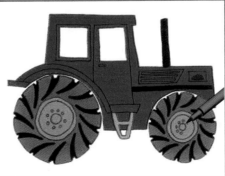

6. Draw a door and a frame around the window. Add a handle on the door. Then, draw a trim, a radiator grill and a vent on the engine.

7. On the wheels, draw curves for the tread, coming in from each half circle. Then, add circles and bolts on the hubcaps, like this.

8. Using a pencil, draw the tractor's driver. Draw over the lines with a thin black pen. Then, fill him in with other pens.

Truck stop

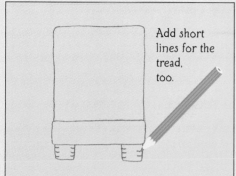

Add short lines for the tread, too.

1. Use a pencil to draw a rectangle for the truck's bumper on pale paper. Then, draw a square above it for the cab, and add two wheels.

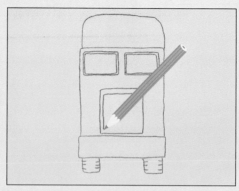

2. Draw a rounded shape at the top, for the top of the trailer. Draw rectangles for windows, too. Then, add a square radiator grill.

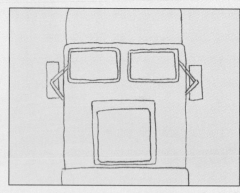

3. For the wing mirrors, draw two bent lines coming from each window. Then, draw a mirror around each pair of lines, like this.

You could draw a truck with big stacks for exhaust fumes.

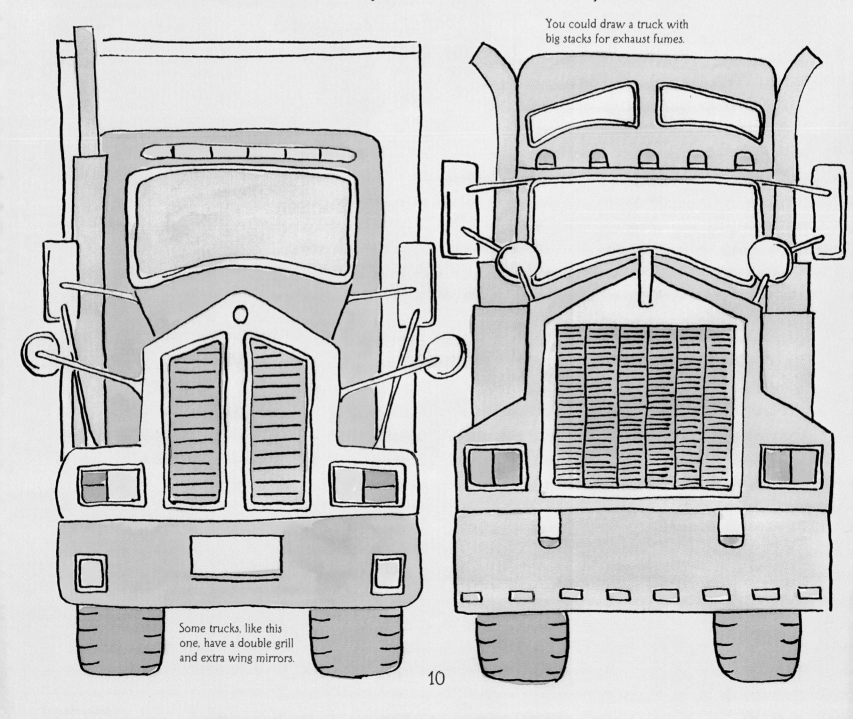

Some trucks, like this one, have a double grill and extra wing mirrors.

Don't worry if you go over some of the lines.

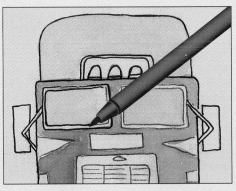

4. Draw headlights on the cab and bumper, and on the trailer. Then, add extra markings on the cab and lots of lines on the radiator grill.

5. Using watery paint, fill in the cab. Paint the trailer, windows, wheels, bumper and lights, too. Then, leave the paint to dry.

6. Carefully draw over all the pencil lines with a thin black felt-tip pen. Then, when the ink is dry, erase any pencil lines that you can still see.

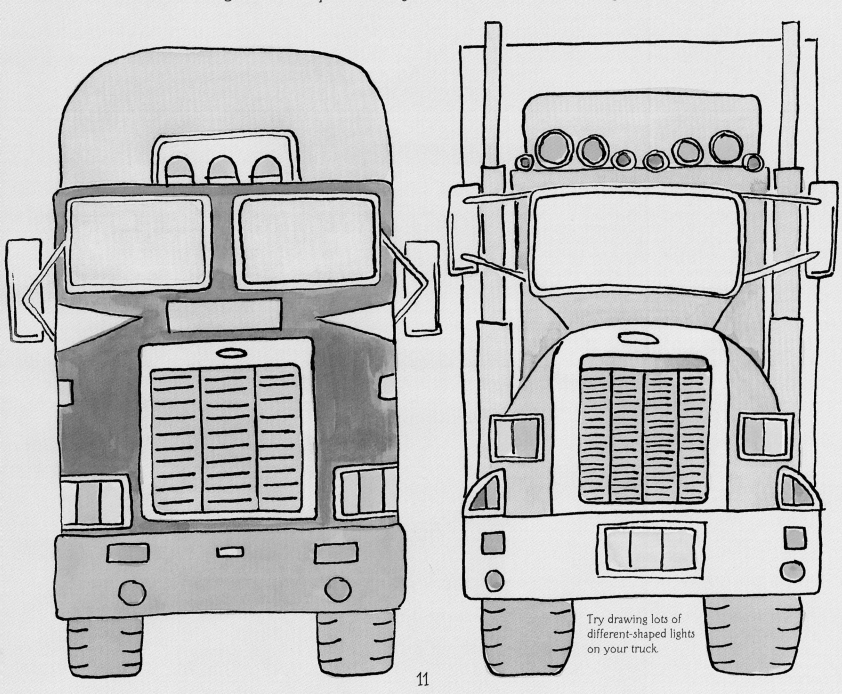

Try drawing lots of different-shaped lights on your truck.

Busy tractor

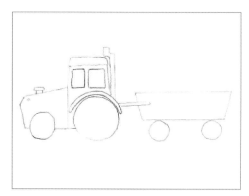

1. Draw two wheels with a pencil, then draw the rest of the tractor. Add stacks at the back and the front. Then, draw a trailer.

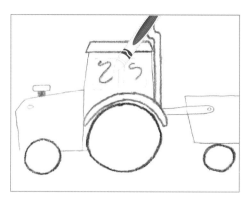

2. Using wax crayons, draw over the outlines shown here. Add blue wavy lines on the window, then fill it in with a white crayon.

3. Draw lines and little round rivets on the tractor and trailer. Then, add hubcaps and V-shaped treads on the wheels.

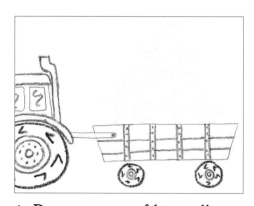

4. Draw a row of big yellow spirals above the trailer, for hay bales. Then, add another row above them, and more rows above that.

The wax crayon will resist the paint.

5. Mix paints with water, to make them runny. Then, paint over each part of the picture and paint yellow ground at the bottom.

To add smoke coming from the stack, draw a swirl with a white wax crayon, then paint over it.

Draw stalks of corn around your tractor with an orange pencil.

6. When all the paint is completely dry, draw little mice between the hay bales with pencils. Add some stalks of corn, too.

In the farmyard

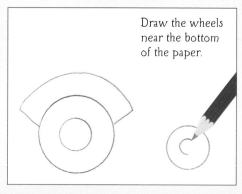

1. Pressing lightly, draw a big tractor wheel on a big piece of white paper. Add a hubcap and a mudguard. Then, draw a smaller wheel, too.

2. Starting at the top of the mudguard, draw a shape for the front of the tractor. Add a stack, then draw a grill on the side and one at the front.

3. Draw a farmer sitting on the mudguard, holding a steering wheel. Draw his head, but don't draw his eye and mouth yet.

4. For chickens, draw small half circles. Add feathers at one end of each half circle, for their tails. Then, draw more feathers for wings.

5. Draw a pointed barn above the tractor. Add a roof, doors and a window, then draw a lock and lots of planks. Add a hedge and other animals.

6. Draw over all the pencil outlines with felt-tip pens. Then, add curved treads on the wheels and bolts on the hubcaps.

7. To fill in the tractor, dip a clean paintbrush into water. Brush in from the outlines, to spread the ink. Then, fill in the rest of the picture.

8. Leave the ink to dry. Then, draw the farmer's face with thin pens. Draw details on the chickens and other animals, too.

9. For the background, fill in all the white spaces with watery brown paint. Leave a white border around each part of the picture, like this.

Try adding a painted sun and sky.

You could add the farmer's wife on another tractor.

Draw curved lines for smoke coming from the stack.

15

Fairground trucks

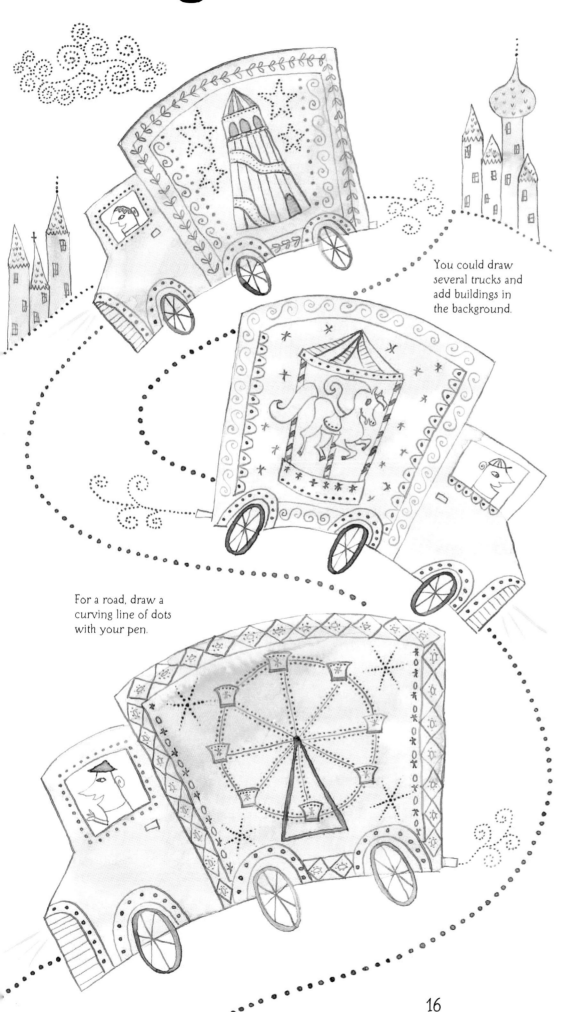

You could draw several trucks and add buildings in the background.

For a road, draw a curving line of dots with your pen.

Use a pencil.

1. Draw a curved rectangle for the truck's trailer, then add a cab. Draw three wheels with mudguards, then add a window and grill on the cab.

Draw spokes on the wheels, too.

2. Fill in the trailer and cab with watery blue paint. Then, when the paint is dry, draw over the lines with an ink pen or thin felt-tip pen.

Decorate the truck with stars, dots and diamonds.

3. Draw a border inside the trailer. Add a ferris wheel in the middle, then decorate the rest of the truck. Draw a driver in the cab, too.

Monster trucks

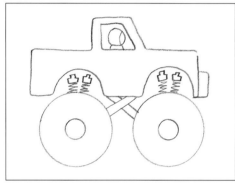

1. Draw a truck, with a cab at the top and wheel arches at the bottom. Add a bumper, then draw two giant wheels, with hubcaps in the middle.

2. Draw a window with a driver inside. Then, draw two shock absorbers above each wheel. Add lines for a crossbar below the truck.

3. Add headlights and a flag. Then, draw patterns on the truck and fill it in with pens. Draw over the outlines with a thin black felt-tip pen.

Parts of these trucks were filled in with a silver felt-tip pen.

Look at these trucks for different ideas of how to draw and decorate a monster truck.

Muddy tractor

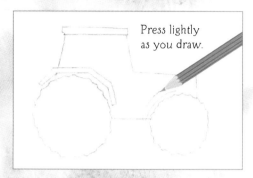

Press lightly as you draw.

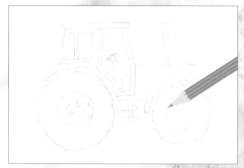

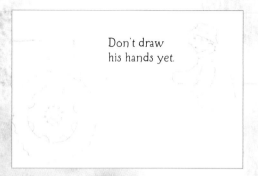

Don't draw his hands yet.

1. Using a pencil, draw two wheels with bumpy treads. Draw the main part of the tractor above the wheels, then add mudguards.

2. Draw a window and a doorway with a steering wheel inside. Add a funnel and steps. Then, draw hubcaps on the wheels.

3. Draw the farmer's hat and jacket, a little way away from the tractor. Draw his face, then add two curved shapes for arms.

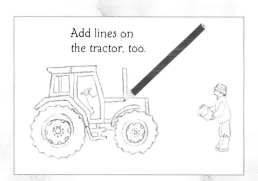

Add lines on the tractor, too.

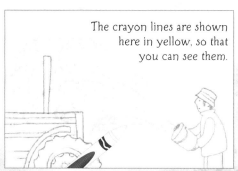

The crayon lines are shown here in yellow, so that you can see them.

4. Draw a bucket in front of the farmer. Make it overlap one of his arms. Then, draw his hands holding onto the bucket, like this.

5. Draw the farmer's legs and add his boots, with bumpy soles. Then, draw over all the outlines with different pencils.

6. Use a white wax crayon to draw lots of lines and swirls of water coming out of the bucket. Add more swirls over the front of the tractor.

The wax resists the paint.

7. Paint the tractor with runny paints. Fill in the farmer, the sky and the grass, too. Then, leave all the paint to dry completely.

8. For mud on the tractor, scrunch up a paper towel and dip it into some brown paint. Then, dab the paint over the tractor.

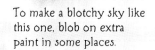
To make a blotchy sky like this one, blob on extra paint in some places.

In the fields

Draw the tractor near the bottom of your paper.

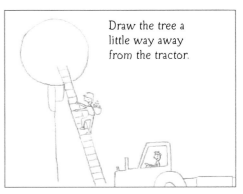

Draw the tree a little way away from the tractor.

1. Pressing lightly with a pencil, draw the cab and engine of a tractor. Draw a window, two wheels, and stacks. Then, add a driver.

2. Draw a trailer behind the tractor and add wheels. Draw two more trailers. Then, join the trailers to the tractor with lines.

3. Draw a circle for a tree, and add a trunk and branches below it. Add a ladder, then draw a man with a basket on his back.

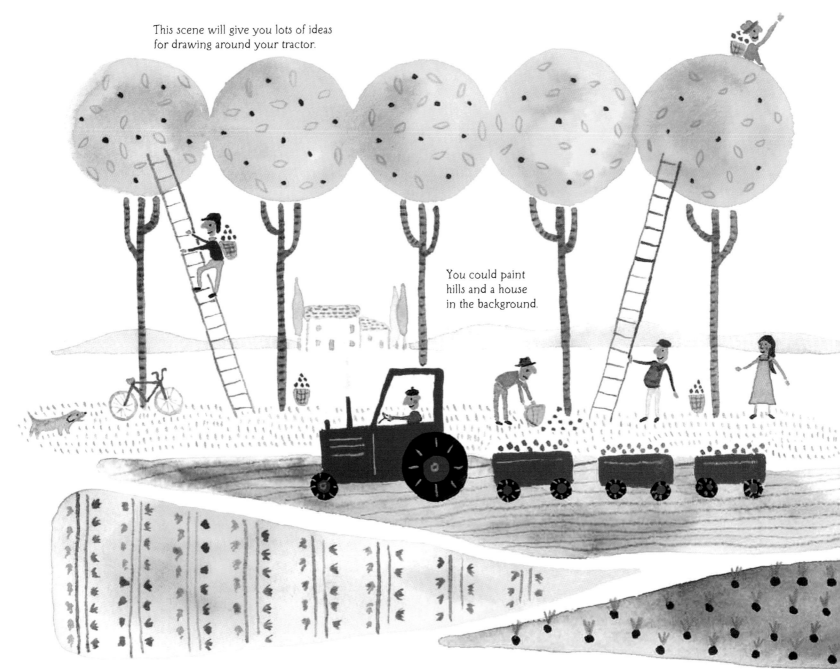

This scene will give you lots of ideas for drawing around your tractor.

You could paint hills and a house in the background.

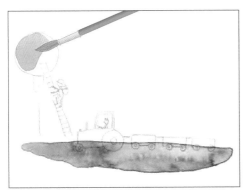

Use the tip of a thin paintbrush.

4. Paint a field with watery brown paint. Don't worry if it overlaps the tractor. Then, paint the tree green and leave the paint to dry.

5. Paint the tractor, trailers, tree trunk and ladder with thicker paint. Paint the driver and the man on the ladder, then leave the paint to dry.

6. Draw faces with a thin black pen. Add lines on the tractor with a white pencil. Draw lines on the field and fruit and leaves on the tree.

Draw lots of apple trees, for an orchard.

If you want to draw
two trucks, draw both
of them before folding
the paper in step 6.

Driving in the rain

Leave a space between the cab and the fold.

1. Fold a piece of dark paper in half, then unfold it again. Draw a truck's cab above the fold, using a cream chalk pastel. Then, fill in the cab.

2. Draw the truck's bumper below the cab with a dark chalk pastel. Fill it in, then add two black wheels below the bumper, like this.

Use dark and light blue chalk pastels for the stripes.

3. Fill in the windshield with a blue chalk pastel. Draw people in the cab, then add some diagonal stripes across the windshield.

4. Draw two side-view mirrors on the cab. Then, add light blue lines for a radiator grill. Draw white and orange headlights, too.

Draw the road below the fold.

5. Draw a dark blue curve, for the road. Add a wider, lighter blue stripe below it. Then, blend the chalks a little with the tip of your finger.

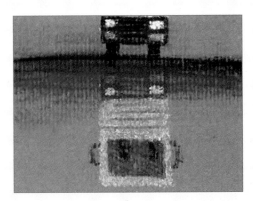

6. Fold the paper again. Rub hard all over it with the back of a spoon. Then, unfold it, to see a reflection of the truck below the fold.

7. Draw white chalk shapes on top of the reflections of the headlights. Then, smudge them down the paper with your finger.

8. To make the truck look as if it is driving in the rain, smudge an eraser diagonally across it several times. Don't press too hard.

9. Dip a dry brush into some runny white paint. Then, pull a finger over the bristles and splatter paint around the wheels, for water spray.

23

Tractor race

1. For the tractor, draw a rectangle on a piece of red paper. Draw a curve across the top right-hand corner. Then, cut out the shape.

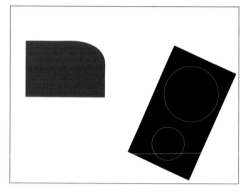

2. Glue the tractor onto a piece of white paper. Then, draw one big wheel and one smaller one on black paper. Cut out both wheels.

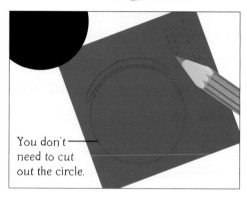

You don't need to cut out the circle.

3. Lay the big wheel on blue paper. Draw around it, then draw a mudguard. Draw two stacks. Cut out and glue on the mudguard and the stacks.

To make a big race like this, glue lots of tractors onto a large piece of paper.

You could draw more than one animal driving a tractor.

You could glue on a piece of green paper for grass, before you glue on your tractors.

Try making a tractor with a winch, like this one.

There are lots of different tractors in this race. Look at them for ideas.

Your tractor could have a trailer with baby animals riding in it.

4. Draw two hubcaps and a seat on red paper. Draw a headlight on yellow paper, too. Then, cut out all the shapes and glue them on.

Draw curls on the sheep's wool.

5. Using a pencil, draw a sheep driving. Add a steering wheel, then go over the lines with a thin black felt-tip pen. Fill in the sheep with pens.

Add a stand for the seat, too.

6. Draw a radiator grill, vents and rivets on the tractor. Add bolts on the hubcaps and curly lines for steam. Then, add more tractors.

25

Going to market

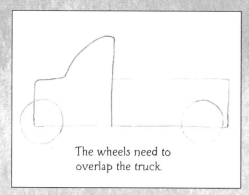

The wheels need to overlap the truck.

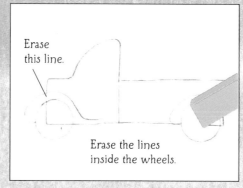

Erase this line.

Erase the lines inside the wheels.

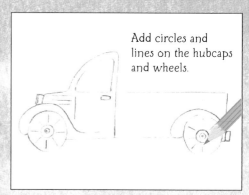

Add circles and lines on the hubcaps and wheels.

1. Pressing lightly with a pencil, draw a shape for the truck's cab. Add a rectangle for the back of the truck, then draw two wheels.

2. Add curved lines for mudguards, over the wheels. Then, erase the lines where the wheels and mudguards overlap the truck.

3. Draw a window and a handle on the door. Add a bumper, and a headlight on the hood. Then, draw a hubcap on each wheel.

Look at this picture for ideas when you're drawing your truck.

To draw bananas, paint a big yellow shape, then draw bananas on top with an orange pencil.

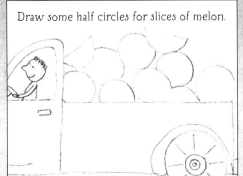

Draw some half circles for slices of melon.

4. Draw a driver in the window and add a steering wheel. Then, draw lots of circles for watermelons in the back of the truck.

5. Fill in the truck with bright runny paints. Paint the wheels with black paint, then fill in the driver and the watermelons.

6. When the paint is dry, draw over all the lines with bright pencils. Add lines on the watermelons and on the back of the truck, too.

You could draw plants or animals in the back of your truck.

27

Semi truck

Start drawing at the right-hand side of your paper.

Add a trim along the trailer, too.

1. Draw the front of the cab. Add a wheel and a window. Then, draw a stack. Add the back of the cab behind the stack.

2. Draw a long trailer behind the cab. Add four wheels at the bottom. Then, draw a fuel tank and steps beneath the cab, like this.

3. Add hubcaps on the wheels and details on the cab and trailer. Then, draw over all the outlines with a black ballpoint pen.

You could draw a rocky desert and road around your truck.

4. Using a white wax crayon, draw a wavy line down the stack. Then, fill in parts of the fuel tank, steps and hubcaps, too.

5. Draw long white whoosh lines along the truck with the crayon. The lines will make the truck look as if it is going fast.

6. Using runny paints, paint the cab and the trailer. Then, paint the wheels and the rest of the truck. The wax will resist the paint.

The crayon lines are shown here in yellow, so that you can see them.

Draw each whoosh line from right to left, like this.

Car transporter

You could draw cars on the transporter that look the same, or lots of different kinds of cars.

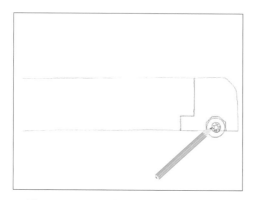

1. Draw two long lines across a piece of paper. At one end, draw a cab, like this. Add a wheel, with a wheel arch and a hubcap.

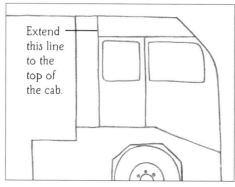

Extend this line to the top of the cab.

2. Draw a line across the cab, near the bottom. Make it slope at one end. Then, draw two windows and a door above the line.

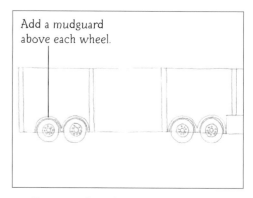

Add a mudguard above each wheel.

3. Draw double lines at each end of the trailer. Add lines in the middle, too. Then, draw two wheels with hubcaps at each end of the trailer.

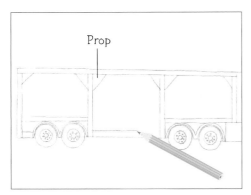

Prop

Sloping rack

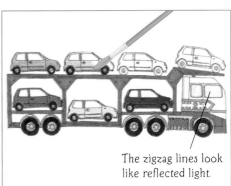

The zigzag lines look like reflected light.

4. Draw another line at the top of the trailer. Add props below it. Then, draw lines above the wheels and across the bottom of the trailer.

5. Draw a sloping rack over the cab. Add little circles for bolts on the props and the racks. Then, draw lots of cars on the racks, like this.

6. Outline the truck and cars with a black felt-tip pen and add details such as zigzag lines on the glass. Then, fill in the picture with pens.

Tractor in the snow

For a snowy landscape, draw hills with trees. Draw more tracks, too.

Draw rabbits in the snow and birds in the trees.

Fill in the driver with pens.

Shake off any excess glitter mixture.

1. Pressing lightly, draw the main part of the tractor. Add two wheels, a mudguard, a window and stacks. Then, add wavy lines for tracks.

2. Brush water on the tractor, but not the window. Blob on watery paint. When it is dry, draw outlines with a thin black pen. Add a driver, too.

3. For glittery tracks, mix sugar with a little glitter. Brush white glue along the tracks, then sprinkle the mixture over the glue.

You could add a dog in the back of the tractor.

Edited by Fiona Watt. Americanisation by Carrie Armstrong. Photographic manipulation by Nick Wakeford.
First published in 2005 by Usborne Publishing Ltd., 83-85 Saffron Hill, London, EC1N 8RT, England www.usborne.com Copyright © 2005 Usborne Publishing Ltd.
The name Usborne and the devices ♀ ⬨ are Trade Marks of Usborne Publishing Ltd.
First published in America in 2005. Printed in Malaysia.